Ladybird Readers

Timmy Loves Football

Notes to teachers, parents, and carers

The *Ladybird Readers* Beginner level helps young language learners to become familiar with key conversational phrases in English. The language introduced has clear real-life applications, giving children the tools to hold their first conversations in English.

This book focuses on the game of football and provides practice of using verbs such as "play" and "kick" in English. The pictures that accompany the text show a range of settings, which may be used to introduce one or two pieces of topic-based vocabulary, such as "walk" and "run", if the children are ready.

There are some activities to do in this book. They will help children practice these skills:

 Speaking   Listening*   Writing   Reading   Singing*

*To complete these activities, listen to the audio downloads available at www.ladybirdeducation.co.uk

Series Editor: Sorrel Pitts   Text adapted by Hazel Geatches   Song lyrics by Wardour Studios

LADYBIRD BOOKS
UK | USA | Canada | Ireland | Australia
India | New Zealand | South Africa

Ladybird Books is part of the Penguin Random House group of companies whose addresses can be found at global.penguinrandomhouse.com.
www.penguin.co.uk   www.puffin.co.uk   www.ladybird.co.uk

Penguin
Random House
UK

First published 2021
001

This book is based on 'Learning Time with Timmy', an English language learning experience for pre-school children including the 'Learning Time with Timmy' courses © British Council 2015; and the 'Learning Time with Timmy' series © Aardman Animations Ltd 2018.

'Timmy Time' and the character 'Timmy' are trademarks used under licence from Aardman Animations Limited.
'Learning Time with Timmy' is a trademark used under licence from Aardman Animations Limited.
britishcouncil.org/english/timmy

Printed in China
A CIP catalogue record for this book is available from the British Library
ISBN: 978-0-241-44013-1

All correspondence to:
Ladybird Books
Penguin Random House Children's
One Embassy Gardens, 8 Viaduct Gardens, London SW11 7BW

Ladybird Readers

Timmy Loves Football

Based on the Learning Time with Timmy TV series
created in partnership with the British Council

Watch the original episode "Timmy's Favourite Things" online.

LEARN MORE!

Watch on ▶ YouTube

▶ YouTube /LearningTimeWithTimmy
LearningTimeWithTimmy.com

Picture words

Timmy

Osbourne

Paxton

Otus

kick   goal

Timmy and his friends are playing football.

Osbourne is in goal.

Paxton kicks the ball.

Does the ball go in the goal?
No! The ball does not go in the goal.

Now, Otus has the ball.

He gives the ball to Osbourne.
Otus! In football, you KICK the ball!

Now, Timmy
has the ball.

Timmy loves football!

Timmy kicks the ball.

Does the ball go in the goal?

No! The ball does not go in the goal.

Timmy is not sad.
Timmy loves football!

1 Talk with a friend.

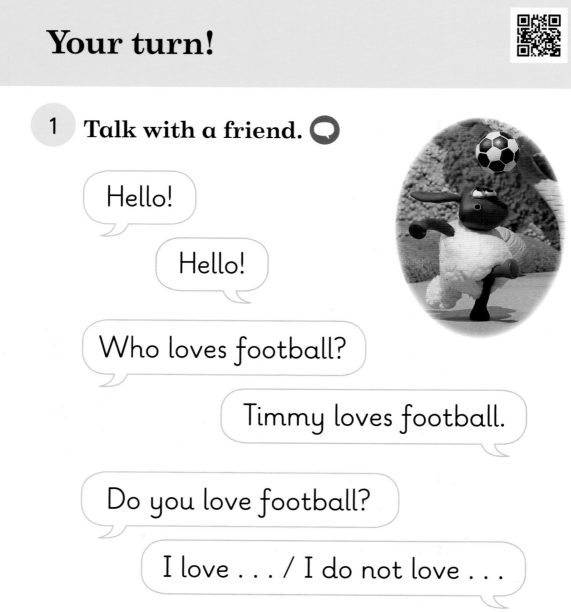

Hello!

Hello!

Who loves football?

Timmy loves football.

Do you love football?

I love . . . / I do not love . . .

2 **Listen. Put a ✓ by the correct words.**

1 a Timmy kicks the ball. ☐

   b Paxton kicks the ball. ✓

2 a Otus has the ball. ☐

   b Timmy has the ball. ☐

3 a Osbourne plays football. ☐

   b Otus plays football. ☐

4 a Timmy has the ball. ☐

   b Timmy kicks the ball. ☐

3 **Listen and read. Match.** 🎧 📖

1 Otus has the ball.

2 Paxton kicks the ball.

3 Osbourne is in goal.

4 Timmy loves football.

4 Listen. Write the first letters. 🎧 ✏️

1  **b**all

2 **g**oal

3 **k**ick

5 Sing the song. 🔊

Timmy kicks the ball.
The ball does not go in the goal.
Paxton kicks the ball.
The ball does not go in the goal.

Well done, Otus! Well done, Osbourne!
Timmy and his friends.
Well done, Timmy! Well done, Paxton!
Timmy loves football!

Ha, ha, ha! Ho, ho, ho!
Timmy loves football!
Ha, ha, ha! Ho, ho, ho!
Timmy loves football!